名流詩叢 35

日出日落
Sunrise and Sunset

李魁賢漢英雙語詩集

我離開淡水時
詩寫淡水
心思留在出生的故鄉

我離開台灣時
詩念淡水
無法斷絕世居的故鄉

我離開世界時
詩留淡水
願終究成為詩的故鄉

李魁賢（Lee Kuei-shien）◎著・譯

前言

　　日出而作，日落而息，人生汲汲營營，盡在此間；詩創作，也盡情於此，甚至日未出早已作，日已落猶未息。

　　自從1963年投入詩創作以來，66年於茲，出版詩集22冊，詩作1243首，一生由少年日出時代，孜孜不倦，迄今已至暮年，面臨日落時刻，還不肯停筆。

　　此集仍照往例，按創作編年方式收錄近兩年詩作，共計64首，採用漢英雙語，旨在配合參與國際詩交流活動，方便與國際詩人交往分享。

　　詩宜由自身表達，其餘不必多所置喙，而詩之分享，也往往不需多言，當可心領神會，一切盡在不言中。

2019.10.28

目次

庫德斯坦

我翻譯過法依克的詩〈圖畫〉

庫德孩童繪男人圖畫

把槍繪在肩膀上

我翻譯過哈巴實的詩〈紅雪〉

雪落在白茫茫的庫德斯坦山脈

立刻變成血紅一片

啊，有過輝煌歷史的庫德族人

委屈生活在流離失守的家園

持槍守衛流血的土地

我呼籲世界敞開胸懷

讓公投尊重各民族自決

文化和生活方式

不要槍　不流血

一票投庫德斯坦獨立
一票投台灣獨立

2017.09.12

淡水榕堤夕照

榕樹鬚根

密集排列簾幕

夕陽隱退幕後

以熱血壯士姿勢

獻出全副能量

給台灣國度生命力

激情照耀半邊天

演出濺血自溺謝幕

壯士畢竟是鳳凰不死鳥

化身大鵬遠飛

仍會按照計畫時程

以獨立形象

再度輝煌台灣大地

2017.09.29

淡水球埔

比鳥飛得更遠的是
沒有翅膀的圓形白球

比眼淚更令人憐惜的是
清晨無人看顧的露珠

比新娘心情更不安的是
等待誰會來肆意踩踏的草埔

比時間更輝煌記錄的是
百年不間斷的人情

2017.10.01

淡水桂花樹

國際詩人結伴蒞臨

亞洲詩人溫文

非洲詩人熱烈

美洲詩人沉著

歐洲詩人從容

在淡水忠寮鄉間道路

共同種植桂花樹

賦予四洲四季體質

夙著文風的忠寮桂花樹古宅

復育成國際詩人桂花鄉

以天為父地為母

桂因詩而貴氣

桂香留在鄉里芬芳

詩因桂而思念

詩韻流傳在詩人心中

播放到世界各處

2017.10.02

淡水詩故鄉

我離開淡水時

詩寫淡水

心思留在出生的故鄉

我離開台灣時

詩念淡水

無法斷絕世居的故鄉

我離開世界時

詩留淡水

願終究成為詩的故鄉

2017.10.03

淡水捷運

進出淡水捷運站的旅客

是什麼樣的人呀

昨日淡水飲食之美

留下一天的味覺餘韻

進出淡水捷運站的旅客

是什麼樣的人呀

今日淡水風景之美

存續一年的視覺映像

進出淡水捷運站的旅客

是什麼樣的人呀

明日淡水詩文之美

寶藏永生的心靈縈懷

2017.10.06

櫻花鉤吻鮭

在雪霸高山

冷冽七家灣溪流中

奮力逆游給妳看

一生反抗外在寒心的鬥志

標示在身上不明顯

不願炫耀的雲紋斑點

妳可以看出櫻花瓣

繁華後留香給本土的心願嗎

要在原生故里傳下後代

以自鱒為榮的傲氣留給後代

把自然基因的本質永存後代

在清流中透澈給妳看

只能在污泥裡殘喘苟延的

外來偷渡雜種

不堪冷受澈骨的磨練時

唯我獨鱒一志

以台灣鮭魚的盛名

建立國際不能磨消的存在

2017.10.29

戲詠水仙百合

說你是水仙，那是假仙

說你是百合，其實不合

你自己獨立存在

不在乎任人分門分類

色彩渲染美是天性

不論如何命名

無關品質和氣質

來自南美移植品種

台灣以好風好水迎接

落土為安心傳種

已酷似我鍾愛的台灣杜鵑

何如正名水仙百合杜鵑

混種再加混名

那真是百合

無疑

2017.10.31

淡水榕樹

——祝賀水源國小百年慶

我是百年老榕樹

一天又一天

看到學生像一群小麻雀

在操場跳躍奔跑

在教室朗朗讀書歌唱

在樹蔭下遊戲結伴

吸收大屯山脈生命的靈氣

我是百年老榕樹

一年又一年

看到學生成為一群大老鷹

在鄉村為生活打拚

在城市為建立基礎盡力

在國外為創造台灣意象盡心
發揮水源活化生命的意義

我是百年老榕樹
依然植根在校園故土
以有限的華蓋範圍
展現無限希望的活動空間
看到一代又一代的孩子
長成社會各界精英
用不斷的鬚根記錄生命的經歷

2018.03.03

五月花組詩

台南鳳凰花

五月新娘

穿起老祖母

當年出嫁的紅衫

喜氣鬧到

全台南熱起來

新娘只是紅著臉

那種紅

叫做羞紅

2018.05.19

新化玫瑰花

壓

玫瑰花

就是不扁

自然風

乾成木玫瑰

硬氣

不折不扣

是金剛不壞乾燥花

2018.05.22

烏山頭南洋櫻花

用心引進南洋櫻

魂卻被南洋接走了

看到默默排隊成

迎神行列

五月是悲情的季節

連素顏的風采

都自動收斂

熱

何其淒切

2018.05.23

噍吧哖杜鵑花

革命魂串連成

一片滿山紅

有緋紅殷紅水紅粉紅

不一樣語族的戰士

血一樣沸騰

融合傳衍

混成自然暈染的紅彩

變化多樣的台灣花色

2018.05.24

台東朝顏

台灣東方聖地

不是後山

是朝向日出的秀臉

素樸朝顏之花*

台灣多種族原生地

熱帶生命靈氣

山林永遠在髮舞

海浪持續在擊鼓

朝活躍在此

晚休息在此

台東給我的第一首詩

竟是一甲子重逢的驚喜

* 朝顏是Morning Glory（清晨的榮光），亦
  稱牽牛花。

2018.05.26

突尼西亞，我的茉莉花呀

茉莉花束夾在我耳上，以清香

向我耳語突尼西亞，柏柏人熱情的原鄉

我無緣親見原始簡樸的岩洞穴居

沿地中海邊綠洲帶，熱夏的涼爽風聲

聲聲迴響腓尼基人建立迦太基的熱情

城堡抵禦不住羅馬人雄壯跨海而來的英武

即使漢尼拔名將最終只有在流亡中嘆息

兩軍彼此以砲火對話，以旗幟招搖

以鮮血互相塗染成顏色一致的屍體

迦太基留下馬賽克永恆的拼貼藝術

羅馬帝國遺址是斷柱殘壁廢墟

茉莉花束夾在我耳邊唏噓

千年歷史種族糾葛萬語也難盡吧

阿拉伯人接踵渡海帶來可蘭經

以深透內心的信仰滋潤沙漠的荒蕪

歷代王朝恩怨起伏有時是宮廷血腥劇

帝國嬗遞更是翻天覆地洗牌

綿延漫長中有淘汰的苦難、有創造的喜悅

人民有時流離失所、有時大量移入定住

動亂成為民族攪拌器，混合出共同的基因

近代引來法蘭西伸手插花又接枝

沙漠之狐也強行侵入捲起滿天沙塵暴

就這樣引導突尼西亞進入20世紀

突尼西亞，我的茉莉花呀

正當台灣陷在白色恐怖歷史羅網中

擺脫殖民地的呼聲發自突尼西亞人民內心

國土台地陣容整齊浩大的橄欖樹以翠綠武裝

捍衛現代突尼西亞天空的獨立與自由

忠貞於季節的鸛鳥沿高速公路

獨立在高壓輸電線高桿頂築巢放哨

獨立，啊！美麗的辭彙喚醒自主的欲求

如今藍白二色建築風景呈現生活的獨立色彩

與地中海輝煌藍天白雲的自由意志相映

茉莉花以玉蘭花的清香吸引我

不辭千里萬里來探訪人類非洲故里

跋涉地理回溯歷史變動風潮

在迦太基故址重建的羅馬古城廢墟

登上巴拉特女神殿振臂高呼

「同胞們，我全心奉獻給突尼西亞！」

地中海沉默給自己聽，蔚藍給自己看

不管海上波浪洶湧或在安靜睡眠

茉莉花束夾在我耳上，受地中海微風撫慰

在我耳邊迴響：啊！突尼西亞

是呀！獨立，是呀！獨立，是呀！

以清香留住永恆美麗的記憶

遠隔重洋傳播回到我的台灣祖國

2018.07.21

淡水是我，我是詩

如果人民沒機會讀詩

我們把詩送到人民面前

如今你可以在進出淡水捷運站時

看到詩貼在牆上對你眨眼

如今你可以在倉庫改建的展覽場

看到詩在窗口反光在地上閃亮

如今你甚至從洗手間解放出來後

可以在詩的面前洗滌一下心靈

如今你可以在廢用的公共電話機旁

讀到詩以遙遠的聲音呼喚你

將來你可以在便利商店買飲料時

詩讓你在透心涼中感到暖和

將來你可以在餐廳點餐時

在餐桌墊紙上讀到難忘的開胃詩

將來你可以在鮮麗慶典式街旗

見識到詩迎風招展你的笑容

將來你可以在舊街購買美食後

把淡水美的詩帶回家咀嚼無窮餘味

我們把詩送到人民面前

人民隨時有機會讀詩

讓淡水真正成為詩的故鄉

因為淡水是我，我是詩

2018.09.12

淡水詩歌節

國際詩人年年來到淡水

共享詩的心靈饗宴

詩人帶來對台灣衷心的愛

淡水以台灣人的熱情回應

大屯山以魁偉體態

觀音山以溫婉身姿

淡水河以潺潺呢喃

台灣海峽以洶洶呼嘯

鳳凰花以熱血奔放

大冠鷲以浪漫翱翔

馬櫻丹以雜色小旗

小麻雀以啁啾細語

共同歌詠淡水內在之美

讓詩的餘韻持續蕩漾

2018.09.21

淡水日出

淡水山崗上運動公園

早起老人做甩手扭腰晨操

連微風都不敢驚動

同樣早起的鳥

被山腳下更早起的車聲壓制

連啁啾二字都說不出口

幾抹白雲劃過藍底的天空

像小孩感冒哈啾

不留心噴嚏流出的鼻水

濺到對面觀音頭上

太陽從大屯山脈小坪頂探頭出來

怒目而視像忍不住氣的金剛

即使有成排黑板樹蕭立在側

即使有台灣欒樹配襯輝煌喜悅

即使有遛狗在草地尋尋覓覓

老人垂目不敢逼視金光

不敢繼續在荒廢公園徘徊

2018.09.22

淡水岸礁

被風刀凌厲雕塑定型

在富貴角燈塔照耀不到的海岸

孤獨經過多少世紀了呀

天空來來往往的飛鳥

荒路上急急飛過的人影

如同空白的日子可數

沒人發現那塊海風催黑的岩礁

經不經心雕鑿成

不再修飾的最後遺作

竟是米開朗基羅聖殤庇祐祂*

五百年前模仿的原型

* 米開朗基羅聖殤（Pieta），又名聖母慟子
　像或哀悼基督，梵蒂岡聖彼得大教堂典藏
　名作。

2018.10.14

給智利的離情詩

聖地亞哥春景

聖地亞哥初春安全島上

不知名的街道樹

把綻放的紅艷花朵

高高掛起一盞盞喜燈

向大地垂顧寒冷後

一絲絲溫暖

像是特別在十月

為循詩人軌跡的慶典

準備報喜的小天燈

回顧人間社會的冷暖

詩人呀

自身冷暖不定的心情

無法安頓的此在

亮起的紅燈

是不是提供了警訊

2018.10.21 Melipilla

近山情怯

從聖地亞哥出城

遠看近禿的山丘

對妳當做無私的天

坦然表露心意

不需再用草木植被

掩飾想說又說不出口

不想說又不想違背

大地自然法則的情意

光禿雖然缺少樹林之茂

近看遠離視非

光自在是自然本質

平坦的草被生機盎然

只是沒有眾樹喧嘩

零落灌木成為孤單標誌

孤獨是詩人自然本質

心自在

免為情煩

2018.10.21 Melipilla

詩飄洋過海

在瓦爾帕萊索

仰望山丘植滿

層層疊疊密集的房屋

聶魯達故居La Sebastiana

廁身在此發射靈性

俯瞰海港水天一色

有大船運貨進來

有大船運貨離去

沒有載運過一首詩

詩自己當會飄洋過海

送進妳冷暖自知的心湖

如果沒有碼頭設備

同樣無法下載

一生心靈的結晶只剩詩

妳要能收存

愛就免費歸妳所有

要不

隨它去吧

任其隨緣飄洋遠揚

2018.10.21 Melipilla

山谷平原

在山谷平原

兩旁山丘稜線浮凸

像是天空無心的摺線

把陽光折攏

滋養翠綠橄欖樹

催熟整齊葡萄園

熱鬧紅橙黃綠藍靛紫花卉

在穿腸而過的柏油路面

車輛朝山谷空隙奔馳

衝向黃昏在前面等待的黑夜

甘願把陽光留給妳

萬物之母的沃野田園

疲於奔命的老朽

理應滿足等候中的黑夜

對亟待安息的人

黑夜最親切

2018.10.21 Melipilla

重臨黑島

再度來到黑島

眺望心情激蕩的海面

妳說不願像海浪

向海岸岩礁敘述衷情

同時擊碎自己

其實岩礁急於收拾

海浪不輕易出口的碎語

散發給全海洋分享

寧願自己不時被沖蝕消瘦

只是禁不住有時回應

提醒妳不要被風言風語

沖離應有方向

不然就只好識時務

自沈海底

讓妳隨意成為平波或急浪

岩礁不需忍耐旁觀

只有仰望

2108.10.21 Melipilla

荒郊墓地

這次又來瞻仰你墓地

依然靜悄悄

詩人文森‧維多夫羅呀

你長年處在此荒郊

是自己的心意

還是不得已

生前有過激情的表現

往生只剩野風在耳邊細語

我來此與你談詩藝

同感讓形容詞死掉吧

但你說詩人是一位小小上帝

果真有那麼神嗎

其實詩人呀

連情人都不想聽你的話

詩人已變成死靈魂

還說什麼上帝

2018. 10 .22 Los Vilos

白楊木

白楊木保持正直的心情

正如正直的姿態

憑身高為妳阻擋不知從何方向

會突襲而來的風勢

以致筆直的軀幹意外側彎

自己默默忍受

不讓妳知覺

經過長年太平日子後

妳已忘記安寧

因為有白楊木衛護

卻開始嫌白目不會彎曲

率直又無趣

為了盡量望遠

又偏偏阻礙到視線

白楊木呀白楊木

2018.10.22 Los Vilos

獨吟勿忘我

在蘭卡瓜的奧斯卡‧卡斯特羅墓地

我吟詩〈勿忘我呀,勿忘我〉悼念

智利詩人彈唱〈勿忘我〉歌曲

眾人隨唱應和

勿忘我呀,勿忘我,盤繞在心裡

即使在妳身邊

勿忘我一直在我心裡盤繞

有些話不敢說，有些字不敢寫

情愛自然會被時間沖淡

不需等到空間的隔離

勿忘我合唱時彼此心心相繫

唯我獨吟時

真的深怕兩情相忘

不再記憶

2018.10.22 Los Vilos

黑島軌跡

在黑島，聶魯達呀

你的詩就是大砲武器

壓制囂張的軍隊

我的詩卻比不上小子彈

嚇不到小鳥

怕反而傷到自己

你的情意時常翻新

始終有人廝守

我的情人時常翻臉

無一日長相左右

聶魯達呀

在你的黑島紀念館

舉辦詩書發表會

不是挑釁，而是歸趨

我再度來到黑島

循詩的軌跡

沒有留下足印

匆匆離去

2018.10.29 返台機上

沉默如石

一心在荒山野地

培植沙漠之花

一心奔馳預定朝聖

米斯特拉爾巨石墓地

我刻意繞到碑後

穿過現實空無

探求非現實的實在

「心靈之於身體

猶如藝術之於人民」*

一心對沉默如石的妳

找尋對話的開口

終究只能在巨石前留影

留下懷念的片刻

把巨石留在身後歷史

獨自黯然彳亍

陪著夕陽

下山

2018.11.01

智利棕櫚

在熱情的智利國土

街道　屋前　山坡　海濱

熱情的棕櫚招展不同風姿

有魁偉的電線杆

有凸肚的酒瓶

有曲線玲瓏的妖嬈

有葉蒂不斷的刺蝟

有鑽地冒出的尖錐

有環肥的釀槽

棕櫚呀棕櫚

離情依依

想像終生的伴侶吧

枝葉不纏綿

這疏離的樣相

原來

即所謂個性

2018.11.02

淡水在我心中

我心中
　　有愛
　　有詩
　　有鄉情

在開心與關心之間
　　　　　愛在
在開心與關心之間
　　　　　詩在
在開心與關心之間
　　　　　鄉情在

愛在

開心與關心之間

　　詩在

開心與關心之間

　　　　鄉情在

開心與關心之間

淡水在我心中

　　有愛

　　有詩

　　有鄉情

2018.12.05

霧台神山

旭出，從獵寮眺望

神山在初晨光輝浸潤下

兀自仰首遙望整夜纏綿後

徐徐離去還割捨不斷的滿月

在寧靜的群山環抱裡

日月同時與我並存

我究竟是誰？受此榮寵

Sabau*！我本是山地的孩子

一生在城市流寓，來此面對神山

感到神魂不知浪蕩在何處

本是族人共存團聚所在

被賦予國名，家反而莫名

我是魯凱族，你是排灣，他是漢

或是我本漢族，你是魯凱，他是排灣

這才是真正台灣一家親

我們有各自族語，又有共同語言溝通

即使在高山上，彼此沒有高山症

日月輝映，似醒還睡

似睡其實早已清醒

在此祖靈地，最幸福的故鄉

                     * Sabau，魯凱族問候語，有「你好、辛苦、
                        謝謝」等意思。

2019.01.24

星圖

仰觀星空

看到像雨後的蜘蛛網

晶瑩珠結間

似有似無的情絲

相連相戀

白天來到七星潭

在美麗腰身的曲線沙灘

俯察細柔的肌理

檢視夜風掃落的星星

都已化成碎石

端詳那些大小不一
　　　形式不一
　　　粗細不一
靜靜袒露姿勢的石子
紋路映現謎樣的星圖

2019.03.07

繆思石雕

橢圓的鵝蛋臉
花梗挺直凸出的鼻子
蓮蓬原生髮
矗立在七星潭旁
眺望水波蕩漾

應該黝黑的肌膚　白啦
本來年輕的鬢髮　銀啦
堅持久遠的記憶　茫啦
不管歷史或不歷史
石頭昂然創造藝術

亂髮原來是捲雲

儼然不動的臉型

不是如山

根本是奇萊山

在我心中圓圓滿滿

2019.03.07

達摩石
——喜戲詩人林豐明

打開你的黑盒子*[1]後

三十年來

你的頭髮竟然也白啦

這究竟是

怎麼一回鳥事*[2]

在你辛酸用詩批判

我當年竟然沒有解讀出

幽默的真性情

你嘻笑表現天然的溫暖

我怒罵算不算是另類幽默

二十年前你贈送我的玫瑰石

依然在書房陪伴我

我賦詩的往事幾乎忘啦

你再度給我的達摩石

彷彿是天地為你雕琢的身影

*1 《黑盒子》是林豐明的第一本詩集。
*2 林豐明一首著名的詩題〈黑百鳥事〉。

2019.03.07

希臘風情組詩

希臘橄欖樹

希臘橄欖園

繁枝不用修剪

好像長滿相思樹

原來醃漬的橄欖

酸酸澀澀

類似愛情相思

對台灣相思

竟然同樣味道

酸酸澀澀

懷念台灣相思樹

2019.04.10 艾維亞島

艾維亞島的天空

陰陰沉著臉

相思卻沉不住

氣雨下

不斷

愛該斷

不斷

又怨又恨

情不晴

就這樣相思連雨

希希拉拉

這真是

希臘

2019.04.10 艾維亞島

希臘古劇場

在埃雷特里亞*

任憑雨愛下不下

任憑風愛吹不吹

任憑陽光愛照不照

6300個席位

滿座是雜草無聲

發不出激昂呼叫

只有場外遍地

紅黃紫白各色化身繁花

用燦爛呼應

古代繁華的激情

那是古代消失的語言

無人聽懂

* 埃雷特里亞（Eretria）是希臘艾維亞島上
  的小鎮，公元前五、六世紀是重要的希臘
  城邦。

2019.04.11 艾維亞島

希臘檸檬黃

在艾維亞島

庭院屋角常見檸檬黃

晶瑩獨霸一方

到處沉默翠綠包圍下

不服氣的野菊黃

不時在呼應吶喊

偶有罌粟紅搶眼

插小花旗招搖

黃就是黃

不理會

有時還裝蒜

依然是黃

保持亮麗的

春景

2019.04.11 艾維亞島

希臘衛城博物館

三十多年來

二度進入雅典衛城

轉進衛城博物館

衛城殘缺歷史影像

博物館重構虛擬全體

真實神殿巨柱

見證過輝煌原貌

繼續臨風臨雨

面臨遊客一再驚豔洗禮

殘缺遺存的零落實體

在空調投射光照耀下

靜靜呈現歷史顯赫

三十多年人間歲月

終究匆匆一瞥

2019.04.16

羅馬尼亞組詩

鐘聲

我在雅西國際書展

念完〈雪的聲音〉

錄音的金髮女郎

來找我合照

她說我的聲音像鐘聲

然而教堂鐘樓附近

鴿群起落如常

不受到鐘聲干擾

原來我的鐘聲是報時鐘

時時提醒自己

時間一點一滴流逝

不論寒暑晴雨

無關心情愉快或鬱悶

我的讀詩聲音只在空中傳播

引不起人間騷動

2019.05.16

詩與歷史

女詩人安潔拉讀〈奉獻〉

說她知道228屠殺事件

那些英靈在詩裡復活了

畢竟詩已勝過歷史

真情贏過虛偽

凸顯掩埋過的真相

我倒是擔心

詩終究也會被虛假的歷史淹沒

她說不用怕

讀〈我的台灣　我的希望〉

你有希望

詩就有希望

2019.05.16

詩人不孤單

另一位女詩人安潔拉

在雅西國際書展會場

聽我朗誦〈樹不會孤單〉

半夜打電話向她丈夫轉述

　天空知道

孤獨的樹

不孤單

詩人正如大大小小的樹木

用詩葉向天空亮票

綴連成一片心靈的翠綠

詩人的本質是孤獨

但存在於人間

顯然

不孤單

2019.05.17

詩公園

和二位安潔拉女詩人

到柯博公園

我探問名稱由來

是地景或是紀念性質

她們不知道

我提議改名安潔拉公園

她們想知道是哪位安潔拉

我說那就叫雙安潔拉公園吧

她們回答：不！

應該稱為李安潔拉

如今在雅西

已經有一座李公園

在二位安潔拉心靈裡

2019.05.18

雅西紀念碑

蕭立在1989年雅西革命紀念碑前

大理石巨大十字架上方

青空無限　白雲悠悠

車輛遠遠停止

禮讓行人輕鬆跨越街道

不必紅綠燈規範

旁邊林蔭下工人在植被草坪

我仰望十字架頂部

陽光閃耀晶瑩

彷彿在台北二二八公園內

蕭立在紀念碑前的心情

同樣流血流汗奉獻給

羅馬尼亞人民和土地的神魂

我滿懷敬仰靜立

白雲悠悠　青空無限

2019.05.24

與埃米內斯庫*1同在

在雅西柯博公園裡

我與你合照

滿地是鬱金香

一區一區不同顏色

擎起詩的旗幟

向天空吶喊

背面有菩提樹屏障

在羅馬尼亞雅典娜神殿

前面廣場上

我站在你身邊

喬治*2歌劇的預演

在空中飄揚

我忽然間想起

台灣。台灣呢?

好像失落什麼?

台灣詩人

歷史上的身影

在哪裡?

*1 米哈伊‧埃米內斯庫（Mihai Eminescu, 1850~1889），羅馬尼亞民族詩人，在雅西卡羅爾一世林蔭大道矗立有巨座立身雕像，柯博（Copou）公園有胸像，在布加勒斯特的羅馬尼亞雅典神殿前面廣場上有立像，其他地方所在都有。
*2 喬治‧安奈斯可（George Enescu, 1881~1955），羅馬尼亞作曲家、指揮家、小提琴家、鋼琴家。

2019.05.31

憑弔尼古拉*

遠從台灣

飛到羅馬尼亞

憑弔你墓地

仰望大理石碑

金字塔型尖頂

陽光閃耀

好像你在天國微笑

我也看到羅馬尼亞30年來

真正解放後

人民臉上陽光的笑容

台灣陰沉沉的天空

卻從我陰沉沉的心底

浮上來

* 尼古拉（Nicolae Popescu, 1937~2010）是
  詩人艾蓮娜‧波佩斯古（Elena Popescu）
  的夫婿，羅馬尼亞學術院院士，代數學泰
  斗，我們2006年在尼加拉瓜結識，不久他
  就前往天國。我到2019年5月19日才有機會
  到布加勒斯特墓園憑弔。

2019.05.31

柯博公園念詩

柯博公園有詩的韻味

百多年前埃米內斯庫

在菩提樹下寫詩

國際詩人如今

聚在他面前

讀詩像樹枝交錯

參天的樹幹從來不因

政權變換而彎曲過

樹葉想遮天

從葉隙間

總有詩

把人間福音

隨光滴落下來

2019.06.03

廣場鞭炮聲

1989年布加勒斯特

革命廣場鞭炮聲

引來辣辣槍聲

槍聲引來

人民忍耐不住的吼聲

吼聲引來

被壓制過久的歷史爆發聲

歷史爆發聲引來

期待民主時代的歡呼聲

歡呼聲引來

男女老幼清脆的笑聲

笑聲引來

國際詩人朗朗的讀詩聲

2019年處處可聞

2019.06.06

遠方

看到妳的時候

妳在遠方

妳回來的時候

還一直在遠方

只有詩

在我身邊

2019.06.06

福山福地福氣

山羌在林邊草地

細嚼幼草

無畏人聲車聲

山猴在樹間飛躍

摘取嫩葉

無視人群圍觀

自然界如此自然

市民嚮往自然

來到福山

享受自然福地福氣

人類這物種

因演化而墮落

不得不匆匆離去

回歸不自然

2019.06.12

外星人遺詩

我的神魂

輕輕離開自己身體

捨不得離別妳的身心

我的神魂在飄蕩

看到妳的花容更孤挺

妳看不到我佝僂的形影

聽到妳的笑聲更春暖

妳聽不到我喉嚨已入冬

我的神魂在太空飄蕩

不占妳的空間

不存在妳的世紀

我變成外星人

神魂獨自

在太空虛無飄蕩

2019.06.13

淡水碼頭錨定樁

你拴得住我的船殼

拴不住我的身體

你拴得住我的身體

拴不住我的心

你拴得住我的心

拴不住天空

2019.07.05

黃昏觀音山

1.

黃昏時

淡水河失落鏡子

天空失落影子

觀音山閉目

不願眼見

人間沉淪黑暗

2.

黃昏時

觀音山點亮

一盞一盞光明燈

映照星圖

引航還要在黑暗中

掙扎的無數生靈

2019.07.06

淡水紫藤園

淡水紫藤花

在純自然清境

綻放貴氣

視覺比美桂華香

以紫色渲染

鋪展春臨大地

像新婚場景

仰望天空

一陣

紫氣東來

來到你我相伴

香伴忠寮

永久的故鄉

2019.07.29

香港天空流淚了

天在看

人在做非人的行為

天天看在眼裡

尚黑集團原來根本

就是用警棍為人民服務

對抗天賦自由人權

舉槍朝人民

射擊的時候

連天空都流淚了

2019.08.13

台灣獨立

實實在在

想過

期待過

評選過

一面旗幟

可攜帶身上

在國際飄揚時

顯示我的獨立人格

標誌台灣獨立的歷史事實

一直在等待中成為虛幻

在國土上找不到認同

國際上受到鼓勵時

虛心到變成心虛

我還是堅持

即使死後

一面旗

代表

台灣

實實在在

2019.09.08

二合一樹

百年土產破布子老樹

昂立在石牆樓門前

儼然保護神

引來麻雀貪婪

把雀榕籽藏在樹凹處

浸久鬚根往下長

子子孫孫一根又一根

霸占破布子根基

像鐵絲拒馬團團包圍

緊縮生長空間

剩下朝天獨撐樹梢

勉力光合

呼吸

2019.10.06

火山情結

墨西哥煙峰

獨立莊嚴的神態

突出雄據天空

黑色岩渣仍霸占

周圍山岡平地

貌似淡水觀音山

獨立安詳的神態

佈置四方青翠山脈

形成綠意大地

墨西哥乾燥的墨面土壤

成就熱情洋溢的民意

台灣深綠舒適的世界

培養善良溫順的民情

山的樣貌

在同情連結中

形成不同連結的詩情

*墨西哥煙峰，是波波卡特佩特火山
（Popocatépetl）的別稱，世界上最活躍的
火山之一。

2019.12.07

人間病態

武夫莽漢病態

眼不見天空流行

中國特色的

一帶一路會員病毒

疫口同聲

台灣是

中國不可分割的一部分

卻拼命一省一省一市一市

封城隔離

分割成獨立實體

正當中國人心震盪時

成都以地震回應

顯示天地人

通通心律不整

2020.02.06

小葉欖仁落葉時

立春後

公園內整排小葉欖仁樹

弱勢小葉變黃

像感染疫病

一陣風起

捲到空中翻滾

紛紛落地

一具一具的葉屍

荒亂棄置於地

完全不像

新社區的新春景象

有待人來收拾

2020.02.20

疫病流行

疫病流行嚴重

從封口

封城

到封關

不能擁抱

不能親嘴

不能對話

即使夫妻

即使情人

即使一家親人

終於

個個分別

成為獨立實體

2020.03.03

青春的蹤跡

詩

青春的文學

旅遊

青春的蹤跡

詩讓我的青春

延續到80歲後的老朽

遍遊五大洲

偶然的生命

來到世界旅遊

最後終站

要永息在台灣

美麗的祖國

2020.05.16

保釋
——悼念詩人趙天儀教授

當年你被警總約談
事先交代
我奔波安排託人
保釋

如今你被神約談
沒有交代
我已經來不及如何
保釋

你還住進天堂
我自閉書房

要探望你

隔著雲端

2020.05.17

詩人簡介

　　李魁賢，1937年生，1953年開始發表詩作，曾任台灣筆會會長，國家文化藝術基金會董事長。現任國際作家藝術家協會理事、世界詩人運動組織副會長、福爾摩莎國際詩歌節策畫。詩被譯成各種語文在日本、韓國、加拿大、紐西蘭、荷蘭、南斯拉夫、羅馬尼亞、印度、希臘、美國、西班牙、巴西、蒙古、俄羅斯、立陶宛、古巴、智利、尼加拉瓜、孟加拉、馬其頓、土耳其、波蘭、塞爾維亞、葡萄牙、馬來西亞、義大利、墨西哥、摩洛哥等國發表。

　　出版著作包括《李魁賢詩集》全6冊、《李魁賢文集》全10冊、《李魁賢譯詩集》全8冊、翻譯《歐洲經典詩選》全25冊、《名流詩叢》38冊、李魁賢回憶錄《人生拼圖》和《我的新世紀詩路》，及其他

共二百餘本。英譯詩集有《愛是我的信仰》、《溫柔
的美感》、《島與島之間》、《黃昏時刻》、《存在
或不存在》和《感應》。詩集《黃昏時刻》被譯成英
文、蒙古文、俄羅斯文、羅馬尼亞文、西班牙文、法
文、韓文、孟加拉文、塞爾維亞文、阿爾巴尼亞文、
土耳其文、德文，以及有待出版的馬其頓文、阿拉伯
文等。

　　曾獲韓國亞洲詩人貢獻獎、榮後台灣詩獎、賴和
文學獎、行政院文化獎、印度麥氏學會詩人獎、吳三
連獎新詩獎、台灣新文學貢獻獎、蒙古文化基金會文
化名人獎牌和詩人獎章、蒙古建國八百週年成吉思汗
金牌、成吉思汗大學金質獎章和蒙古作家聯盟推廣蒙
古文學貢獻獎、真理大學台灣文學家牛津獎、韓國高

麗文學獎、孟加拉卡塔克文學獎、馬其頓奈姆‧弗拉謝里文學獎、秘魯特里爾塞金獎和金幟獎、台灣國家文藝獎、印度普立哲書商首席傑出詩獎、蒙特內哥羅（黑山）共和國文學翻譯協會文學翻譯獎、塞爾維亞國際卓越詩藝一級騎士獎。

2002年、2004年、2006年三度被印度國際詩人團體提名為諾貝爾文學獎候選人。

Foreword

Starting to work when sunrise and gong to rest after sunset, all human being in common are almost spent in this life style. The creation of poetry is about the same, even more, the work has been done quite a while before sunrise and still unrest after sunset.

I have endeavored my poetry creation for 66 years since 1963, and published 22 books of poetry in total amount to 1243 poems. Since my juvenile sunrise era, I have been creating poems tirelessly. Up to date I am so old to face the sunset in my life and yet unwilling to stop writing.

This collection includes 64 poems created within recent years and, as usual, compiled chronologically. By

Mandarin-English bilingual version, it is for the purpose to facilitate sharing with international poets when I participated international poetry festival in recent years.

Poetry should be expressed by itself, and the rest need not be overstated. Moreover, the sharing of poems is frequently realized by responsive souls without too much explanation. That is all.

2019.10.28

Kurdistan

I translated Sherko Faiq's poem "Picture",

in drawing the picture of a man

the Kurdish child drew the gun on his shoulder.

I translated Hussein Habasch's poem "The Red Snow",

the snow comes down white covering Kurdistan's
    mountains

it becomes red soon.

Ah, the Kurds having their glorious history

now spend their aggrieved life in displacing homes

armed with guns to quard their bleeding land.

I call for the world opening the mind

let the referendum to respect self-determination of all
    nations

selecting their own culture and lifestyle.

No gun, no bleed,

one vote to Kurdistan Independence

another vote to Taiwan Independence.

2017.09.12

Tamsui Sunset at Banyan Bank

Fibrous roots of Banyan trees

suspend densely as a wide curtain.

Sunset retreats behind the curtain

with a posture of ardent youth

dedicating his full energy

to the national vitality of Taiwan,

shines half the sky by passion,

performs splashed blood and drown in the end.

After all, the ardent youth is a Phoenix

incarnated into a big bird flying far away,

yet still according to the schedule

making the land of Taiwan glorious once again

with an image of Independence.

2017.09.29

Tamsui Golf Course

What flying farther than the bird

is the white round ball without wings

What more pitiful than tears

is the morning dewdrops that nobody cares about

What more disturbing than the bride's mood

is the grass wandering who will come to tread on

What more brilliant than record

is the human feelings uninterrupted for a hundred years

2017.10.01

Osmanthus in Tamsui

International poets come together to visit us

Asian poets in gentle

African poets in enthusiastic

American poets in calm

and European poets in easy.

We walk over the country paths in Zhongliau village

and plant Osmanthus trees along the paths

sharing seasonal qualities from four continents.

The ancient house in the name of Osmanthus remains

    literary

and resurrected as a hometown of international poets,

there the sky as father and the earth as mother.

The Osmanthus becomes noble due to poetry

with its fragrance staying in the countryside forever,

while the poetry is memorized due to Osmanthus

with its verse circulating in the hearts of poets

broadcasting to all over the world.

2017.10.02

Tamsui, the Hometown of Poetry

When I leave Tsmsui

my poetry describes about Tamsui

minds the hometown of my birthplace

When I leave Taiwan

my poetry remembers Tamsui

forgets not the hometown of my ancestors

When I leave the world

my poetry remains in Tamsui

wishes to become the hometown of poetry.

2017.10.03

Tamsui Mass Rapid Transit

What kind of passengers who

get in and out of the Tamsui MRT station?

The delicious foods of Tamsui yesterday

left an aftertaste for one day.

What kind of passengers who

get in and out of the Tamsui MRT station?

The beautiful scenery of Tamsui today

will remain a visual memory for one year.

What kind of passengers who

get in and out of the Tamsui MRT station?

The precious verses about Tamsui tomorrow

will be persisted as treasure in all life forever.

2017.10.06

Formosan Landlocked Salmons

On the Snow and Papak high mountains

the salmons swim at the best in reverse of the stream

in the cold Cijiawan River,

displaying their intention in lifelong to resist the
external chill.

From the cloudy spots marked on their body

that is not obvious and not to flaunt,

you can see the petals-like of cherry blossoms,

are that aimed to remain for native land after prosperity?

In order to pass on the posterity in the aboriginal
hometown

with the proud of salmon self-pride

to preserve the essence of natural genes forever

they present to be seen through in the clear stream.

When the smuggled alien hybrids

had to spend their residual life in the sludge,

the salmons exclusively insist their sole will

in the name of famous Formosan landlocked salmons

to establish an existence without replaceable internationally.

2017.10.29

Parody to Narcissus Lily

Say you are a Narcissus, it must be a fake fairy.

Say you are a Lily, actually it doesn't.

You exist independently

without care about the classification,

the natural beauty is rendered colorful.

No matter how it is named

irrelevant quality and temperament,

this species transplanted from South America

is greeted by appropriate Taiwan atmosphere.

Rooted on the good earth here peacefully for generations

it's like my favorite Taiwanese Azalea.

Why not entitled Narcissus Lily Azalea?

This hybrid and mixed name

really means good combination

without doubt.

2017.10.31

Tamsui Banyan Tree

— *For Centennial celebration of Shuiyuan Primary School*

I am a banyan tree of one hundred years old

day after day

have watched the students like a group of sparrows

jumping and running on the playground

reading and singing in the classroom

playing games under my shade

absorbing the aura of the Datun Mountains.

I am a banyan tree of one hundred years old

year by year

have watched the students becoming a group of eagles

fighting for life in the village community

doing their best in building the foundation in the city

dedicating their efforts to create Taiwan image abroad

performing the significance of water source to activate

life.

I am a banyan tree of one hundred years old

having still rooted in the homeland of the campus,

displaying an active space for boundless hope

with just a limited circumference under canopy,

watching the children generation after generation

growing into the elites in various fields of society

recording the procession of life by means of fibrous

roots.

2018.03.03

May Flowers

Flame Flower at Tainan

May bride

wears the red wedding dress

used by old grandmother long ago.

The happiness is spread

to heat up entire Tainan city.

The bride blushes to a red face,

that kind of red is called

shy red.

2018.05.19

Roses at Xinhua

The roses

would not be flatten

by pressure,

yet dried by natural wind

to become wood roses

that hardened to

complete dried flowers

as stiff as steel.

2018.05.22

Gliricidia at Wushantou

He endeavored to transplant Gliricidia into Taiwan

while his soul was summoned to Southeast Asia.

The Gliricidia in rows silently are looked like

the God greeting parades.

May is the season of sadness

even ordinary make up

is automatically suppressed.

Hot

so unhappy.

2018.05.23

Azalea at Tapani

The revolutionary souls are interconnected

to become red all over the mountains,

there are bright red, dark red, pale red, rose red.

The warriors from different tribes

have same boiling blood

in hybrid to bear new generation,

interpenetrated as a new natural red color

a variation of Taiwanese color shade.

2018.05.24

Morning Glory at Taitung

Holy land at eastern Taiwan

is not backside of the mountain

rather the nice face fronting sunrise,

a plain flower of morning glory.

On this multi-racial native land In Taiwan

with tropical aura of life,

the forest is dancing constantly

the waves are smashing consistently.

I act here by day

and take rest here at night.

The first poem that Taitung inspires me

is a big surprise for encounter again after 60 years.

2018.05.26

Oh, Tunisia, my machmoum!

Machmoum, a bouquet of jasmine, is clipped on one
of my ears
whispering with fragrance of Tunisia, the hometown
of passionate Berbers,
though I have no chance to see the aboriginal rock
cave.
Along the Mediterranean coast and oasis, the fresh
breeze of the hot summer
echoes with enthusiast Phoenicians building Carthage.
The castle couldn't defend the heroic Romans who
came across the sea,
even Hannibal the Great at last couldn't but sigh in
exile.

Opposite armies entrenched in gunfire swayed with

flags and

painted with blood on each others' bodies in a uniform

color.

Carthage today is an eternal mosaic collage in the

museums,

and the Romans remain as broken pillars and collapsed

walls in ruins.

The machmoum clipped beside one of my ears is

sighing for

the millennial history of ethnic entanglement so difficult

to express.

The Arabs subsequently came across the sea bringing
the Coran

to console the barren desert with religious beliefs
penetrating into deep heart.

The transformation of the dynasties plays a bloody
drama of the court

and the change of the empires is even more thoroughly
overturned.

During long-term history there are suffering from
falling and joy of rising.

People are sometimes exiled and sometimes emigrate
in large numbers.

Turmoil becomes a national blender to mix up a
common gene.

Then, the contemporary French invaded the land and
  exploited the resources,
the desert fox also entered by force and rolled up a
  series of dust storms.
Tunisia was thus guided into the XX century.

Oh, Tunisia, my machmoum, the bouquet of jasmine!
When Taiwan was falling into the historical trap of
  white terrorism
the call to get rid of the colonies came out of the
  hearts of the Tunisians.
The vast array of olive trees in the plain fields is
  armed with emerald greens

in defending the independence and freedom of the modern Tunisian sky.

The storks loyal to the seasons nest and stand sentinel along the highway

independently on the high poles of high-voltage transmission lines.

Ah, independence! Beautiful vocabulary awakens autonomous desire.

Now the blue and white two-color architectures present the authentic essence

reflecting the free will of the Mediterranean brilliant blue sky and white clouds.

Jasmine attracts me with the fragrance similar to the
magnolia's one.

I come from afar thousands of miles to visit the human
homeland in Africa

tracing the geography of mapping the waves in
historical changes.

On the ruins of the ancient Roman land, at the site of
Carthage

I climb onto the Bharat Temple and wave my hands to
shout:

"Countrymen! My heart is totally dedicated to Tunisia!"

The Mediterranean hears itself in silence, and looks at
itself in blue,

irrespective of the waves on the sea being turbulent or
sleeping quietly.

The machmoum is clipped on one of my ears,

caressed by the Mediterranean breeze and resounds in
that ear of mine:

"Oh! Tunisia! Yes! Independence, yes! Independence,
yes!"

for keeping the eternal and beautiful memories with a
fragrance

remotely spread across the ocean and back to my
Taiwanese motherland.

2018.07.21

Tamsui is me, yet I am poetry

If the people have no time to read poetry

we present the poetry in front of the people.

Now, you can see the poetry posted on the wall

    blinking at you

when get in and out of the Tamshui MRT station.

Now, you can see the poetry reflected on the ground

    through windows

when enter the exhibition hall rebuilt from the

    warehouse.

Now, you can refine your mind in front of the poetry

when drain yourself and liberate out of toilet.

Now, you can hear poetry calling from afar

when stand by the disabled public telephone booth.

In future, you can feel warm refreshed by poetry

when buy a drink at any convenience store.

In future, you can read an unforgettable appetizing

     poetry on the table pad

when order your meal at the restaurant.

In future, you can watch the poetry displaying your

     smile by the wind

when look at the vivid street flags for festival

     celebration.

In future, you can bring the poetry home to enjoy

     aftertaste frequently

when buy foods from the Tamsui old street.

We present the poetry in front of the people

let people could read poetry at any time

in order to establish Tamsui as the real homeland of

poetry

because Tamsui is me, while I am poetry.

2018.09.12

Formosa Poetry Festival at Tamsui

International poets come to Tamsui annually

to share the poetry festival among the souls.

The poets bring with their wholehearted love to
Taiwan

while Tamsui responds with Taiwanese enthusiasm,

by a sturdy posture of Datun Mountains

by a gentle gesture of Guanyin Mountain

by a whispering murmur of Tamsui River

by a whistling roar of Taiwan Strait

by a intense blooming of Flame Trees

by a romantic soaring of Crested Serpent Eagle

by a colorful flag waving of Common Lantana

by a pleasant chirping of small sparrows.

All praise the inner beauty of Tamsui

keeping the created poetry lingering for long.

2018.09.21

Sunrise at Tamsui

On the sports park at Tamsui hilltop

an old man who got up early is doing morning exercise,

even the breeze is not disturbed.

The birds that also get up early

unable to sound any chirping because

suppressed by the noises of cars that got up earlier.

A few white clouds pass across the blue sky

like the snivel drained due to sneeze carelessly

by a child catching cold and splashed

onto the crest of Guanyin mountain at opposite bank.

The sun comes out of one hilltop of the Datun Mountains

glaring upon the earth, like an unbearable King Kong.

Even if there are rows of green maple standing beside

even if there are golden-rain trees enhancing the joys

    of glory

even if there are straying dogs wandering on the

    grasses,

the old man does neither dare to glance the glittering

    sunshine

nor to linger in the abandoned park any longer.

2018.09.22

Shore Reef at Tamsui

It has been sculpted by sharp wind

for many centuries, set alone on the coast

that the Cape Fugui Lighthouse does not illuminate.

Flying birds coming and going in the sky

and shadows of people flashing over the deserted path

are infrequent like the leisured days.

No one found that the reef rock darkened by sea breeze

has been inadvertently carved into

a last sculpture without modified any longer,

which is supposedly turned out to be the prototype of

Pieta, a greatest work five hundred years ago by

Michelangelo.

2018.10.14

Farwell Poems to Chile

Spring Landscape at San Diego

On refuge island of San Diego streets

the unknown trees at early spring time

raise brilliant blooming red flowers high enough

like the celebrating lights one by one.

After looking at the cold in the earth

a little by little of warmth

similar to sky lanterns, especially, in October

prepares to inform the world

for celebration of the poetry festival

to reward the fickleness of human nature.

Ah, Poet

your inconstant feeling

is unable to settle Dasein,

then does the lit red lights

give you an alarm for warning?

2018.10.21 Melipilla

Approaching to the Mountain

Out of town from San Diego

I look from afar at the almost bare hill

that calmly expresses its feeling to you

as a selfless sky,

it is not necessary to have vegetation

to conceal its passion

that cannot speak out what wants to say,

and doesn't want to say what is contrary to the natural

    law.

It is looked like lack of prosperous forest

but appeared quiet different to approach.

The light exists itself being the natural essence,

the grassy plain is vital

simply without rustling among trees.

Hardly ever shrub becomes a symbol of alone

and loneliness is the natural essence of a poet

whose soul is rather easy and

free from trouble caused by love affair.

2018.10.21 Melipilla

Poetry Across the Ocean

At Valparaiso

I looked up at the hills planted

with layered houses densely.

La Sebastiana, the former residence of Neruda,

is situated hereabout to radiate a spirituality.

I overlook the harbor, sea and sky in same color.

There are big ships transporting cargos in,

there are also big ships transporting cargos out,

but none of poetry is carried therewith.

The poetry itself will cross the ocean

sent into the lake of your self-conscious heart.

Yet it is unable to be unloaded

if there is no wharf equipment provided.

My literary harvest of all life remains simply poetry

you can possess it freely

just only to receive it,

otherwise

let it be,

let it be gone with the wind crossing the ocean.

2018.10.21 Melipilla

Plain in the Valley

On the plain in the valley

its ridges at both hillsides protrude

like the unintentional fold line of the sky

to enclose the sunshine inside

for nourishing the green olive trees

promoting ripeness of vineyards

and blooming red orange yellow green blue violet

flowers.

On the intestine asphalt pavement passing through the

valley

the car ran towards the mountain pass,

rushing to the dusk followed by the dark night

willing to leave the sunshine to you

the fertile fields of the Mother Nature.

As an old man I am tired of running about

thus should be satisfied with the greeting night.

For those who are in need of rest

the night is most welcomed.

2018.10.21 Melipilla

Returning to Isla Negra

Returning to Isla Negra

I overlook the exciting ocean.

You said you don't want similar to the wave

revealing its mind to the coastal reef

at the price of crushing yourself.

In fact, the rock reef is eager to pick up

the fragments that hardly spoken out by the wave

and to distribute them sharing with whole ocean,

itself would rather be scrubbed from time to time,

just can't help but sometimes respond

to remind you not rushing away

from the direction by rumor.

Otherwise, it has to find the better timing for

self-sinking into the abyss

and let you feel free to become an easy wave or a surge.

Rock reef does not have to suppress itself as a bystander

just only to look up to you.

2108.10.21 Melipilla

The Graveyard at Deserted Suburb

I come back to visit your graveyard again,

here still silent.

Ah, poet Vicente Huidobro,

You have been laying in this deserted suburb for long

at your will

or you have no choice.

Passionate performance during his lifetime

in the past, only the wild wind is whispering in the ear.

I am here to talk to you about poetry.

Let the adjective die with the same feeling.

But you said that the poet is a little God.

Is it really so God?

Actually, the poet

Even the lover doesn't want to hear from you.

The poet has become a dead soul

no matter what God.

2018. 10. 22 Los Vilos

The Poplar

The poplar maintains a sense of integrity

just as its straight posture

to protect you from invaded by storm

coming from all directions with its height.

It must endure itself silently

in the accidental bending pain of its trunk

and to avoid your notice.

After a long period of peaceful days

you have forgotten your serene life

thanks to guard by poplar,

while you start to complain it being straightforward

without sense of bowing and also boring

even hindering your sight

to watch as far as possible,

poplar, oh, poplar!

2018.10.22 Los Vilos

Solo Recital of Forget Me Not

On the graveyard of poet Oscar Castro in Rancagua

I recite his poem "Forget Me Not"

a Chilean poet plays the song "Forget Me Not"

everyone hum following him.

Forget me not, oh, forget me not, is sounded in my heart

even just beside you

"forget me not" has been sounding in my heart.

When it dares not to say something, dares not to write

   some words,

love feeling will be naturally be reduced by time

waiting for not separation in space.

"Forget me not" resounds among the persons in chorus

but when I recite alone

it is really afraid of forgetfulness to each other

no longer to remember.

2018.10.22 Los Vilos

The Track to Isla Negra

Oh, Neruda, on the Isla Negra,

your poems are the strong cannon weapon

against the arrogant army.

My poems are as week as small bullets

not enough to scare the birds,

may on the contrary to hurt myself.

Your affection is often refreshed

accompanied by someone all the times,

my lover frequently disputes with me

not stayed beside me one day long.

Oh, Neruda,

at your Memorial Hall on Isla Negra

we launch new books of poetry

not for provocation, but praise.

I come to the Isla Negra again

on the track of poetry road

and hurry away

without footprints left.

2018.10.29

As Silence as Stone

Devoted myself to plant the flowers

on the desert of barren hills,

Devoted myself to rush at the scheduled pilgrimage

to the graveyard of Mistral Gabriela,

I deliberately walked around the monument

passing through the real vacancy

to search for an unreal essence:

"What soul does for the body

just like artist for the people"*

Devoted myself to you as silence as stone

looking for an opening in dialog,

after all, I could only take a photo in front of your

    monument

left behind the moment for memory

and left the monument behind the history.

I walked alone depressingly

accompanied by the sunset

down the hill.

* The verse by Mistral Gabriela engraved on her
  monument:
  Lo que el alma
  Hace por su cuerpo
  Eslo que el artista
  Hace por su pueblo

2018.11.01

Chilean Palms

On the passionate Chilean territory,

streets, houses surroundings, hillside, seashores,

the passionate palms display different styles,

some look like sturdy electric poles

some look like flagons

some have curvaceous enchantment

some look like spiny hedgehogs

some have sharp cones upright on the ground

some look like fat fermentation tanks.

Palms, oh, palms

I cannot bear to part with you

as my lifelong companion.

Your leaves do not lingering

and this independently spreading status

is turned out to be

so-called personality.

2018.11.02

Tamsui in My Heart

In my heart

    there is love

    poetry

    local affection.

Between happiness and concern

                love exists,

between happiness and concern

                poetry exists,

between happiness and concern

            local affection exists.

Love exists

between happiness and concern,

      poetry exists

between happiness and concern,

         local affection exists

between happiness and concern.

Tamsui in my heart possesses

    love

    poetry

    local affection.

2018.12.05

Vedai God Mountain

At dawn, from the hunter cottage,

I look over the God Mountain bathed under morning
   glory,

it looks up the full moon reluctant to leave slowly

after affectionate passion together over night.

Surrounded by peaceful mountains

the sun and the moon coexist with me at the same time.

Who am I? Given such honored.

Sabau*! I was a child grown up in the mountainous
   village

have been living in the city for a lifetime, now make
   no sense

about where I am in front of the God Mountain.

Here has been where the aboriginal tribe lived together

the family becomes inexplicable when a modern

    country name was given.

Either I am Rukai, you are Paiwan, he is Han,

or I am Han, you are Rukai, he is Paiwan,

this is really one family in Taiwan.

We have respective languages and communicate with

    common one.

Even in the mountains, none is suffered from mountain

    disease.

Sunshine reflects moonlight. I wake up yet sleepily.

It seems sleepiness but actually is waken

in this ancestral land, the happiest hometown.

* Sabau, a greeting of Rukai's language, with
various meanings of "hello, well done, thank
you" and so on.

2019.01.24

Star Atlas

I look up to the starry sky

like the spider webs after the rain.

Among the crystal pearls

it seems that there are love feeling

interconnected or not.

Coming to Seven Stars Lake by day

I overlook at the delicate texture

on the curved beach with beautiful waistline.

The stars swept fallen by the wind during night

have been turned into pebbles.

Those pebble stones with different sizes

          different shapes

          different dimensions

laying naked silently on the beach display

each mysterious starry atlas on its streaked surface.

2019.03.07

Muse Stone Sculpture

It erects on front of Seven Star Lake

with goose egg-like oval face

pedicel-like straight protruding nose

lotus seedpod-like fair

looking over the waves up and down.

It should be dark skin, now becomes white.

It was originally young curl fair, now becomes silver.

It persists the memory for long, now becomes vague.

Regardless of history or non-history

the stone creates the art work standing strictly.

Its chaotic fair is turned out to be cirrus,

its solemn face pattern

does not as immovable as a mountain

but just the Mount Chilai,

round and full perfect in my heart.

2019.03.07

Dharma Stone

—a parody to poet Lin Feng-ming

Since opening your Black Box*[1]

thirty years ago

your hair has become white.

What is going on

the matter something about a bird accident*[2]?

From the bitter criticism by your poem

I did not realize and interpret that year

your real humorous nature.

Your laughing shows your natural warmth

while my curse in rage might be not an alternative

       humor.

The Rhodonite that you presented to me twenty years

ago

has been placing by my side in my study,

I have almost forgotten my creation of poetry for it.

You give me again a Dharma stone

with a form carved naturally according to your figure.

*1 "Black Box" is the title of first book of poetry
by Lin Feng-ming.
*2 "A Bird Accident" is the title of a famous
poem by Lin Feng-ming.

2019.03.07

Greek Exotic Poems

Greek Olive Trees

In Greek olive groves

the prosperous branches without trimming

seem full of acacia growing up.

The pickled olives are turned out

to be sour

similar to love sick.

Nostalgia for Taiwan

has the same taste

to be sour.

I miss Taiwan Acacia when I stay in Greece.

2019.04.10 at Avia, Greece

The Sky of Avia

The sky has an overcast face,

my nostalgia can't stand it.

I blame the rain

why uninterrupted.

Love affair should be interrupted

yet uninterrupted too.

The affection is unclear

keeping resentful and hate,

as such, nostalgia in accompany with rain

pitter-patter, pitter-patter.

This is really

in Greece.

2019.04.10 Avia

Ancient Greek Theatre

In Eretria*

regardless of raining or not

regardless of wind blowing or not

regardless of sunshine or not

6,300 seats of the ancient Greek theatre

are full occupied by silent weeds

without any excited shouting.

Only outside of the theatre

there are incarnated red, yellow, purple and white

　flowers

responding in full bloom

to that ancient flushing passion.

That is the disappeared ancient language

no one understands.

* Eretria is a small town on the island of Avia,
Greece, an important Greek city-state during
5~6 BC.

2019.04.11 Avia

Greek Lemon Yellow

In Avia

lemon yellow is frequently found in the courtyard

occupying brilliantly a part of it.

Surrounded by silent emerald green everywhere

unyielding wild chrysanthemum yellow

shouts from time to time in response,

occasionally, there is poppy red stealing the show

by waving a lot of colorful small flags.

Yellow is just keeping yellow

and ignores other colors,

even sometimes pretending blind.

It is still yellow color

to keep a vivid bright

spring landscape.

2019.04.11 Avia

Greek Acropolis

Since thirty years

I have visited the Acropolis twice,

now, I transfer to the Acropolis Museum.

Acropolis has lost complete history images

while Museum is reconstructing virtual entirety.

The real temple pillars at site

witnessed the brilliant original construction

and continuously exposed to wind and rain

baptized repeatedly by the wondering tourists.

Fragments remained partly in the Museum

present glorious history silently

under the projecting lights air conditioned.

More than 30 years in life

after all, catches a glimpse only.

2019.04.16

Romanian Poetry Sequence

Bell Rings

After I recited my poem "The Sound of Snow"

at Librex Book Fair in Iasi, Romania,

the blonde in charge of live recording

asked me to take a photo with her

and said that my sound is like a bell ring.

However, near the church bell tower

a flock of pigeons rise and fall as usual

undisturbed by the bell.

It turns out that my bell ring is the chime

reminding myself from time to time.

However, time passes little by little

no matter of cold, hot, sunny or rainy

regardless of the feeling being pleasant or unpleasant,

my sound of poetry recital only broadcasts in the air

would not cause any social turmoil.

2019.05.16

Poetry and History

Poetess Angela Furtuna read my poem "Dedication"

saying that she knew the 228 massacre accident

those martyrs have been resurrected in the poem.

After all, poetry has surpassed history,

true fact overcomes hypocrisy

disclosing the buried truth.

But I am worried about

poetry will be overwhelmed by false history at last.

She said no need to be afraid

just read your another poem "My Taiwan, My Hope".

So that only you have hope

poetry has hope too.

2019.05.16

The Poet does not Lonesome

At Librex Book Fair in Iasi, Romania,

poetess Angela Baciu listened to me

reciting my poem "Trees Would not be Lonesome",

called her husband in the midnight quoting

    "The heaven knows that

    lonely tree is always

not lonesome."

Poets are of course similar to various kinds of trees

showing their poems as leaves voting for the sky

to spread emerald green in the souls.

The essence of the poets is loneliness

but their existence in the world

obviously

does not lonesome.

2019.05.17

Poetry Park

I came to Copou Park

in accompany with two poetesses called Angela,

asking about the origination of park's name

whether from the place or in a certain memory.

It was no answer

so I suggested to change it as Angela Park.

Someone asked which one Angela?

I said for both Angela.

They said, no,

should be better Lee-Angela.

Now, there is a park in the name of Lee

within the hearts of two Angela.

2019.05.18

Iasi Revolutionary Monument

I stand in front of the 1989 Iasi Revolutionary Monument,

there are limitless blue sky with relaxing white clouds

above the erected huge marble cross.

The vehicles stop far temporary

waiting pedestrians crossing over the streets at easy

without necessary of traffic lights to restrain.

The laborers are renewing the lawn under the shade.

The sun shines brightly,

I look up to the top of the cross

with same mood as stood in front of the monument

erected in 228 Park at Taipei,

respecting to the same spirits dedicated their blood

and sweat

to the Romanian people and the land.

I stand still in front of the Monument,

there are relaxing white clouds in limitless blue sky.

2019.05.24

In Accompany with Mihai Eminescu*1

At Copou Park in Iasi

I took a photo in front of you.

All over the ground there are tulips

with different colors in respective area

raising the banners of poetry

shouting towards the sky,

linden trees stand as barrier on your back side.

On the square in front of

Romanian Athenaeum in Bucharest

I stood by your side

the singing of George's Opera*² in rehearsal

waves in the air.

I suddenly thought about

Taiwan. What about Taiwan?

It seems something lost?

Where are

the historical figures of

Taiwanese poets?

*¹ Mihai Eminescu（1850~1889）, a Romanian
   national poet whose giant statue is erected on
   the Carol I boulevard at Iasi, a bust in Copou
   Park, another statue on the square in front of
   the Romanian and many in other places.

2019.05.31

Worship before Nicolae's Graveyard

Far from Taiwan

I flied to Romania

for worshipping before your graveyard.

I looked up at the marble monument

brilliant sun rays shine

on its pyramid spire

like you are smiling in heaven.

I also noticed that since 30 years

after real liberation of Romania,

people's smile like sunshine.

At the moment,

the gloomy sky of Taiwan floats upwards

from the bottom of my gloomy heart.

> * Nicolae Popescu（1937~2010）is the late
> husband of poetess Elena Popescu, a member
> of the Romanian Academy, a master scholar
> in algebra field, whom I met in Nicaragua
> in 2006. I did not have the opportunity to
> worship before his graveyard in Bucharest
> until May 19, 2019.

2019.05.31

Poetry Recital at Copou Park

Copou Park has an atmosphere of poetry.

Eminescu wrote poems under the big linden tree

more than a hundred years ago.

Now, a lot of international poets

gathered in front of his bust

reading poems crossed like branches.

The towering trunk has never been bent

due to the regime changed.

The leaves try to hinder the sky

yet from the gaps

there is always poetry

dropping gospel for human being

following after the sun rays.

2019.06.03

Firecrackers on the Square

The firecrackers on Revolution Square

in Bucharest 1989

attracted thrilling gunshots,

the gunshots attracted

the roaring that people can't self-control,

the roaring attracted

a historical burst that has been suppressed for long,

the historical burst attracted

the cheers of expecting a democratic era,

the cheers attracted

joyful laughter of all ages,

the laughter attracts

poetry recitals by a lot of international poets

that can be heard here and there in 2019.

2019.06.06

In the Distance

When I watched you

you are in the distance,

when you come back

you till remained in the distance,

only poetry

by my side.

2019.06.06

Lucky Mountain

Formosan barking deer in the grassland

chew new sprouted grass

ignoring any human and vehicle noise.

Formosan rock-monkeys leaping among trees

pluck new green leaves

ignoring the crowd around.

Nature is so natural

that the visitors yearn for.

I came to Lucky Mountain

enjoying the blessings of nature.

Such a human species

have been corrupting due to evolution.

So the visitors had to hurry away

returning to un-nature.

2019.06.12

Alien Left Poetry Behind

My spirit

quietly departs my own body

reluctant to leave your entity and mind,

and is drifting away lonely.

I watches your flowery figure more proud and straight

while you can't see my bent shadow.

I heard your laughter more spring fresh

while you can't realize my throat at stiff winter.

My spirit is drifting to outer space

without occupying your position

without existent at your century.

I became an alien,

my spirit alone

drifting nowhere in space.

2019.06.13

Rope Stock at Tamsui Dock

You can hold my hull

but can't hold my body.

You can hold my body

but can't hold my heart.

You can hold my heart

but can't hold the sky.

2019.07.05

Guanyin Mountain at Dusk

1.

At dusk

Tamsui River lost its mirror,

the sky lost its shadow too.

Guanyin Mountain closed its eyes

unwilling to see

the surrounding being drown into dark.

2.

At dusk

Guanyin Mountain lights up

Illuminating Lamps one by one

in reflective of star map

to navigate countless creatures

still struggling in the dark.

2019.07.06

Wisteria Garden at Tamsui

The wisteria flowers at Tamsui

bloom a noble atmosphere

in this pure natural fresh circumstance

visually superior than fragrance of Osmanthus

and render with purple color

spreading over the land of spring

decorating as a wedding scene.

When look up to the sky

you will notice

a stream of purple air eastwards

in accompany with you and me

fragrantly staying at Zong-liau village,

our eternal hometown.

2019.07.29

Hong Kong Sky is Crying

The sky is watching

human that are doing inhuman behavior

with big eyes every day.

The partisanship turns out

to serve the people by police batons

against innate freedom and human rights.

When they shoot

towards the people

even the sky is crying.

2019.08.13

Taiwan Independence

I am really

thought

expected

selected

to have a flag

be carried on my body

when waving internationally

just showing my independent personality

displaying the historical facts of Taiwan independence.

I have been waiting so long to become illusory

without identity to be found on the land.

When I am encouraged internationally

my modest heart becomes uneasy.

I will still insist my intention

even after my death

it will have a flag

representing

Taiwan

really.

2019.09.08

Two-in-one Tree

One giant centennial indigenous Bird Lime Tree

stands in front of the stone wall gate

as a protect God.

Flocks of sparrows are attracted to hide greedily

the seeds of Red Fruit Fig in the tree recesses.

After long the fibrous roots have grown downwards

generation after generation

overtaking the foundation of the Bird Lime Tree

surrounding all over like barbed wires.

Its growth space has been threatened

and only its independent treetop skywards

can remain photosynthetic

breathing.

2019.10.06

Volcano Complex

Mexican Smoking Mountain

erects on the high sky

in a solemn independent gesture.

Black scoria still dominantly spreads

all over surrounding hills and flats.

It is looked like Guanyin Mountain at Tamsui

which extends green surfaces along all directions

in a serene independent gesture

to form an greenish land over all.

The blacken surfaced dry soil in Mexico

achieves the passionate people,

while deep green world in Taiwan

cultivates a kindness and gentleness.

The appearance of mountains

displays different poetic connections

in a sympathetic complex.

* Mexican Smoking Mountain, alias Popocatépetl volcano, is one of the most active volcanoes in the world.

2019.12.07

Morbidity on the Earth

The boorish fellows have morbidity

without noticing an epidemic disease spread over the sky

the Chinese characteristic virus

through the country members covered under Belt and

    Road Initiative,

and speak in epidemic unison:

Taiwan is

an inseparable part of China,

while desperately separate provinces and cities one by

    one

by isolation and closing the borders

to become respective independent entities.

When the Chinese people are in shock

Chengdu responds with earthquake

in displaying the heaven, earth and human being in

China

all suffered from arrhythmia.

2020.02.06

When the Leaves of Madagascar Almond Fall

After the Festival of Spring Coming

Madagascar Almond trees in the park

turn their weak leaflets into yellow

as if infected with epidemic disease

and then blown into air

by a gust of wind.

The leaflets are like corpses

fallen one after another

wasted on the land

completely dislike

a new spring scene in New Community

that to be cleared away by someone.

2020.02.20

Virus Pandemic

The virus pandemic is so severe

that from masking the mouths

to closing the cities

and further closing the borders.

People can't embraces to each other

no kisses

no talk

even between the couples

the lovers

or the family members.

Eventually

each individual

becomes an independent entity.

2020.03.03

Whereabouts of Youth

Poetry

the youth literature,

tourism

the whereabouts of youth.

Poetry makes my youth extended

to over 80 years old age

for traveling across five continents.

My accidental life

came to travel to this world

until the last stop

eternal rest place in Taiwan

my beautiful motherland.

2020.05.16

On Bail

— *A monody to poet prof. Chao Tien-yi*

When interviewed by the Security Headquarters

　　many yeas ago

you asked me

rushing to find someone able to request for

a release on bail.

Now interviewed by God

you ask me nothing

so that I have no time to think about how to request for

a release on bail.

You have been settled into the Heaven

while I prisoned myself in my library

I can only visit you

across the clouds.

2020.05.17

About The Poet

Lee Kuei-shien(b. 1937)began to write poems in 1953, became a member of the International Academy of Poets in England in 1976, joined to establish the Taiwan P.E.N. in 1987, elected as Vice-President and then President of it, and served as chairman of National Culture and Arts Foundation from 2005 to 2007. Now, he is Vice President for Asia in Movimiento Poetas del Mumdo(PPdM)since 2014, the organizer of Formosa International Poetry Festival. His poems have been translated and published in Japan, Korea, Canada, New Zealand, The Netherlands, Yugoslavia, Romania, India, Greece, USA, Spain, Brazil, Mongolia, Russia, Latvia, Cuba, Chile, Nicaragua, Bangladesh, Macedonia, Turkey

Poland, Serbia, Portugal, Malaysia, Italy, Mexico and Morocco.

Published works include "Collected Poems" in six volumes, 2001, "Collected Essays" in ten volumes, 2002, "Translated Poems" in eight volumes, 2003, "Anthology of European Poetry" in 25 volumes, 2001~2005, "Elite Poetry Series" in 38 volumes, 2010~2017, and others in total more than 200 books. His poems in English translation include "Love is my Faith", 1997, "Beauty of Tenderness", 2001, "Between Islands", 2005, "The Hour of Twilight", 2010, "20 Love Poems to Chile", 2015, "Existence or Non-existence", 2017, and "Sculpture & Poetry", 2018. The book "The Hour of Twilight" has been

translated into English, Mongol, Russian, Romanian, Spanish, French, Korean, Bengali, Serbian, Albanian and Turkish, and yet to be published in Macedonian, German, and Arabic languages.

Awarded with Merit of Asian Poet, Korea(1993), Rong-hou Taiwanese Poet Prize, Taiwan(1997), World Poet of the Year 1997, Poets International, India(1998), Poet of the Millennium Award, International poets Academy, India(2000), Lai Ho Literature Prize, Taiwan(2001)and Premier Culture Prize, Taiwan(2002). He also received the Michael Madhusudan Poet Award from the Michael Madhusudan Academy, India(2002), Wu San-lien Prize in Literature, Taiwan(2004), Poet Medal from Mongolian

Cultural Foundation, Mongolia(2005), Chinggis Khaan Golden Medal for 800th Anniversary of Mongolian State, Mongolia(2006), Oxford Award for Taiwan Writers, Taiwan(2011), Award of Corea Literature, Korea(2013), Kathak Literary Award, Bangladesh(2016), Literary Award "Naim Frashëri", Macedonia(2016), "Trilce de Oro", Peru(2017), National Culture and Arts Prize, Taiwan(2018), Bandera Iluminada, Peru(2018)and Prime Poetry Award for Excellence by Pulitzer Books, India(2019), Literary Award for Translation from Association of Literary Translators of Montenegro(Udruzenje knjizevnih prevodilaca Crne Gore) (2020), International Award "A Knight of the First Order of Noble Skills in Poetry" from "Raskovnik" Literary and

Artistic Association, Smederevo, Serbia(2020).

He was nominated by International Poets Academy and Poets International in India as a candidate for the Nobel Prize in Literature in 2002, 2004 and 2006, respectively.

Contents

語言文學類　PG2419　名流詩叢35

日出日落Sunrise and Sunset
——李魁賢漢英雙語詩集

原　　　著 / 李魁賢（Lee Kuei-shien）
譯　　　者 / 李魁賢（Lee Kuei-shien）
責 任 編 輯 / 許乃文
圖 文 排 版 / 周妤靜
封 面 設 計 / 劉肇昇

發 　行 　人 / 宋政坤
法 律 顧 問 / 毛國樑　律師
出 版 發 行 / 秀威資訊科技股份有限公司
　　　　　　114台北市內湖區瑞光路76巷65號1樓
　　　　　　電話：+886-2-2796-3638　傳真：+886-2-2796-1377
　　　　　　http://www.showwe.com.tw
劃 撥 帳 號 / 19563868　戶名：秀威資訊科技股份有限公司
　　　　　　讀者服務信箱：service@showwe.com.tw
展 售 門 市 / 國家書店（松江門市）
　　　　　　104台北市中山區松江路209號1樓
　　　　　　電話：+886-2-2518-0207　傳真：+886-2-2518-0778
網 路 訂 購 / 秀威網路書店：https://store.showwe.tw
　　　　　　國家網路書店：https://www.govbooks.com.tw

2020年9月　BOD一版
定價：290元
版權所有　翻印必究
本書如有缺頁、破損或裝訂錯誤，請寄回更換

國家圖書館出版品預行編目

日出日落 : 李魁賢漢英雙語詩集 = Sunrise and sunset
　　/ 李魁賢著. -- 一版. -- 臺北市：秀威資訊科技,
　2020.09
　　　面；　　公分. -- (名流詩叢 ; 35) (語言文學類 ;
PG2419)
　　中英對照
　　BOD版
　　ISBN 978-986-326-844-4(平裝)

863.51　　　　　　　　　　　　　　　　109012091

讀者回函卡

感謝您購買本書，為提升服務品質，請填妥以下資料，將讀者回函卡直接寄回或傳真本公司，收到您的寶貴意見後，我們會收藏記錄及檢討，謝謝！
如您需要了解本公司最新出版書目、購書優惠或企劃活動，歡迎您上網查詢或下載相關資料：http:// www.showwe.com.tw

您購買的書名：_____

出生日期：_____年_____月_____日

學歷：□高中 (含) 以下　　□大專　　□研究所 (含) 以上

職業：□製造業　□金融業　□資訊業　□軍警　□傳播業　□自由業
　　　□服務業　□公務員　□教職　　□學生　□家管　　□其它_____

購書地點：□網路書店　□實體書店　□書展　□郵購　□贈閱　□其他

您從何得知本書的消息？

　□網路書店　□實體書店　□網路搜尋　□電子報　□書訊　□雜誌
　□傳播媒體　□親友推薦　□網站推薦　□部落格　□其他_____

您對本書的評價：（請填代號　1.非常滿意　2.滿意　3.尚可　4.再改進）

　封面設計____　版面編排____　內容____　文／譯筆____　價格____

讀完書後您覺得：

　□很有收穫　□有收穫　□收穫不多　□沒收穫

對我們的建議：_____

_____

_____

_____

11466
台北市內湖區瑞光路 76 巷 65 號 1 樓
秀威資訊科技股份有限公司　　　收
　　　　　BOD 數位出版事業部

....

（請沿線對折寄回，謝謝！）

姓　　名：＿＿＿＿＿＿＿＿＿　年齡：＿＿＿＿　性別：□女　□男

郵遞區號：□□□□□

地　　址：＿＿＿＿＿＿＿＿＿＿＿＿＿＿＿＿＿＿＿＿＿＿

聯絡電話：(日)＿＿＿＿＿＿＿＿＿＿　(夜)＿＿＿＿＿＿＿＿＿＿

E-mail：＿＿＿＿＿＿＿＿＿＿＿＿＿＿＿＿＿＿＿＿＿＿